Pebble® Plus

MAKE IT MINE

Kid Style

SWEET SHOES FOR YOU!

by Megan Cooley Peterson

Consulting editor: Gail Saunders-Smith, PhD

CAPSTONE PRESS
a capstone imprint

Pebble Plus is published by Capstone Press,
1710 Roe Crest Drive, North Mankato, Minnesota 56003
www.capstonepub.com

Library of Congress Cataloging-in-Publication Data
Peterson, Megan Cooley, author.
Kid style. Sweet shoes for you! / by Megan Cooley Peterson.
pages cm.—(Pebble Plus. Make It Mine)
Summary: "Full-color photographs and simple text describe easy
ways to personalize shoes"—Provided by publisher.
Audience: 5-8.
Audience: Grade K to 3.
Includes bibliographical references.
ISBN 978-1-4765-3968-3 (library binding)
ISBN 978-1-4765-6031-1 (ebook pdf)
1. Shoes—Juvenile literature. 2. Boots—Juvenile literature. 3.
Handicraft—Juvenile literature. 4. Decoration and ornament—Juvenile
literature. I. Title. II. Title: Sweet shoes for you!
TT678.5.P48 2014
685.31—dc23   2013035765

Editorial Credits
Jeni Wittrock, editor; Tracy Davies McCabe, designer; Svetlana Zhurkin,
media researcher; Jennifer Walker, production specialist; Sarah Schuette,
photo stylist; Marcy Morin, photo scheduler

Photo Credits
All photos by Capstone Studio/Karon Dubke

Printed in the United States of America in North Mankato, Minnesota.
092013   007775CGS14

TABLE OF CONTENTS

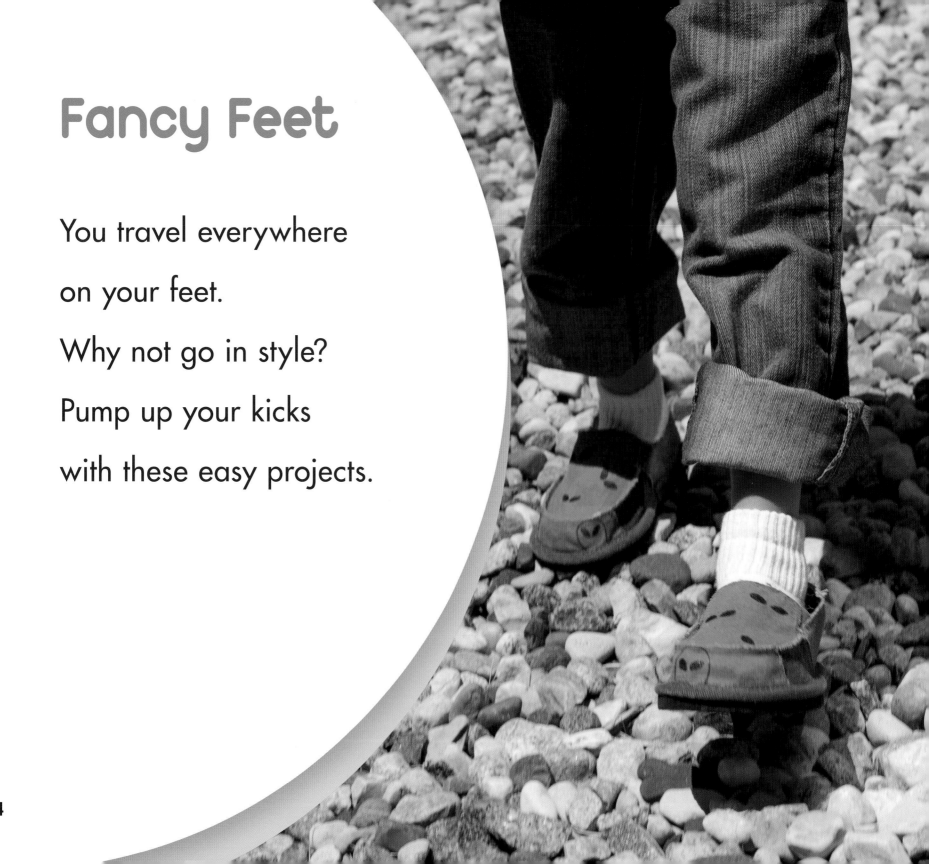

Fancy Feet

You travel everywhere
on your feet.
Why not go in style?
Pump up your kicks
with these easy projects.

Many of the supplies
for these projects
can be found at home.
Other supplies can be
purchased at a craft store.

Basic Tools list:

- scissors
- fabric markers
- foam brush
- decoupage glue
- glitter
- paintbrush
- acrylic paints
- felt
- felt glue

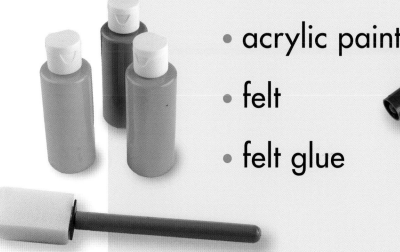

Shoe Bling

Nuts from the garage

become bling on your shoes!

Paint them your favorite colors

or leave them silver.

Let your style sparkle.

May I Have Your Autograph?

Turn canvas shoes

into walking autographs!

Have the superstars

in your life sign

your shoes.

Sparkling Soles

Don't forget to deck out your soles. First paint decoupage glue along the soles' edges. Then sprinkle glitter on the glue. Let it dry.

Alien Kicks

Why celebrate Halloween only once a year? Glowing paint turns your shoes into walking nightmares. Draw spooky faces with a black marker. Boo!

Recycled Laces

Don't toss those old clothes!
Turn your old shirts
and jeans into shoelaces.
First, unlace your sneakers
and set them aside.

Using your shoelaces as a guide, cut two long, thin strips of fabric. Lace up the fabric strips to give your sneakers a fresh look.

Good Dog

Strut down the street with puppies that go wherever you do! First, trace the toe of your shoe on a blank piece of paper.

Use the pattern as a guide.

Cut out heads, ears,

and noses from the felt.

Use felt glue to stick

the pieces to your shoes.

Take It to the Next Level

Step out in a pair of boots as special as you are. Follow these steps or make your own creation. Using your imagination is the best part!

Step 1: Choose pictures you like from glossy magazines, or print out pictures of your family, friends, or even your pets from a laser printer. Cut out pictures with a scissors.

Step 2: Set your boots on a piece of newspaper. Using a foam brush, paint decoupage glue on a small area of one boot.

Step 3: Place a picture on the glue. Use your fingers to smooth out any wrinkles.

Step 4: Repeat steps 2 and 3 until boots are covered with pictures. Let them dry.

Step 5: Paint decoupage glue over the tops of the photos. Let the glue dry.

Read More

Kenney, Karen Latchana. *Super Simple Art to Wear: Fun and Easy-to-Make Crafts for Kids.* Super Simple Crafts. Edina, Minn.: ABDO Pub. Company, 2010.

Meinking, Mary. *Stylish Shoes for the Crafty Fashionista.* Fashion Craft Studio. Mankato, Minn.: Capstone Press, 2012.

Wrigley, Annabel. *We Love to Sew: 28 Pretty Things to Make: Jewelry, Headbands, Softies, T-shirts, Pillows, Bags, & More.* Lafayette, Calif.: C & T Publishing, 2013.

Internet Sites

FactHound offers a safe, fun way to find Internet sites related to this book. All of the sites on FactHound have been researched by our staff.

Here's all you do:

Visit *www.facthound.com*

Type in this code: 9781476539683

Check out projects, games and lots more at
www.capstonekids.com

Word Count: 225
Grade: 1
Early-Intervention Level: 18